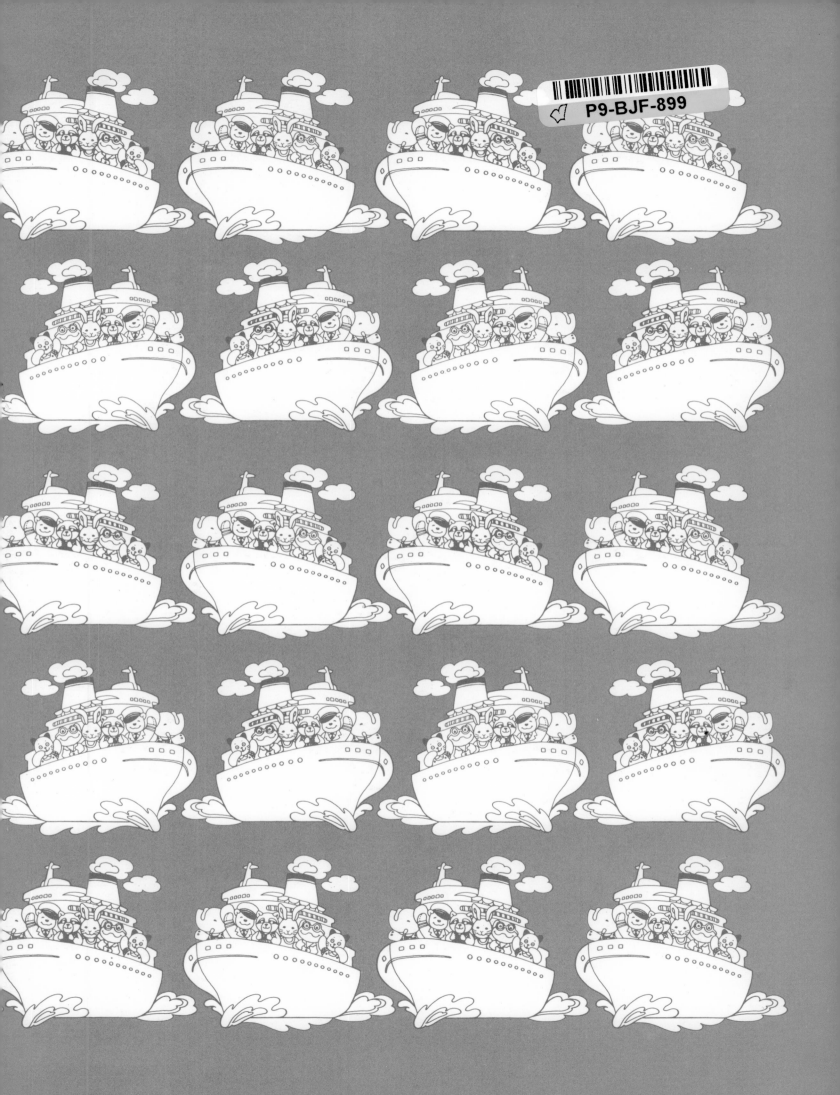

The Second Adventure of the S.S. Happiness Crew:

MYSTERY IN THE MIDDLE OF THE OCEAN

By June Dutton

Illustrations by Eric Hill

Determined Productions, Inc.
San Francisco

Other books in the S.S. Happiness Crew series
by June Dutton, illustrated by Eric Hill:

The First Adventure of the S.S. Happiness Crew:
Cap'n Joshua's Dangerous Dilemma.

© 1981 by Determined Productions, Inc.
World Rights Reserved
Published by Determined Productions, Inc., San Francisco, California
Printed in Hong Kong
Library of Congress Card Catalog No. 81-65682
ISBN: 0-915696-48-7

The S.S. HAPPINESS is sailing smoothly across the Pacific Ocean bound for China, the first stop on a round-the-world cruise.

Cap'n Joshua is standing on the bridge looking out to sea through his binoculars when suddenly he hears, "CAP'N JOSHUA, CAP'N JOSHUA! I MUST TALK TO YOU AT ONCE — SOMETHING MYSTERIOUS IS GOING ON ABOARD THIS SHIP!"

Startled, the Captain turns quickly almost dropping his binoculars overboard. Facing him is Chef Jambon, the Chief Cook. Jambon is terribly upset. He's holding on to his tall chef's hat to keep it from blowing into the ocean. So Cap'n Joshua leads him into the wheelhouse and says, "Calm yourself, Chef Jambon, and tell me WHAT mysterious things are going on aboard our ship!"

"There's a THIEF aboard, sir!" Chef Jambon is so flustered his face is bright red instead of pink.

"A THIEF? How do you know? What has been stolen?"

2

"Many things," replies Jambon. At first it was little things — a box or two of crackers — then a jar of peanut butter — a very LARGE jar. Then the thief made off with a drumstick from the turkey I roasted for Sunday's supper.

"But all that's NOTHING compared to what happened just now!

"A few minutes ago the top layer — with all the lovely chocolate fudge frosting — vanished from my beautiful chocolate cake. When THAT happened, I knew I had to come to you for help. The thief MUST BE CAUGHT IMMEDIATELY!"

3

"We are in luck," Josh says, trying to calm the excited chef. "It's true, we have a mystery. But we also have someone who solves mysteries. Sir Rex, the famous English detective and Chief Inspector from Scotland Yard, is on board.

"He told me when we sailed from San Francisco that he looked forward to great adventures on this cruise. It seems an adventure has already begun.

"Don't worry any more, Chef Jambon. Sir Rex will find the thief. Everything's going to be fine. Now get back to your kitchen and repair that chocolate fudge cake—I want a BIG piece at dinner."

4

Cap'n Joshua isn't very upset. In fact, he's still chuckling when Tasha, the ship's Entertainment Director, rushes into the wheelhouse crying, "Something TERRIBLE has happened, Cap'n Joshua!"

"What now? Don't tell me your gown for tonight's costume ball has disappeared!" The Captain smiles as he teases Tasha.

But Tasha doesn't laugh. Instead she wails, "Miss Lola's JEWELS have been STOLEN. THERE'S A DANGEROUS THIEF ABOARD THE S.S. HAPPINESS!"

"Quiet down, Tasha. Don't alarm the whole ship. Everything's going to be fine." Actually, Cap'n Joshua isn't so sure that everything's going to be fine. "This is a very strange thief," he thinks. "First, crackers and peanut butter, now priceless jewels. What next?"

He looks at the unhappy Tasha and says, "Ask Sir Rex to come to my cabin as fast as possible." Tasha hurries away.

When Sir Rex arrives, Joshua apologizes. "I'm sorry to bother you during your vacation, Sir Rex, but you were asking for adventure—now we HAVE it!" Cap'n Joshua is very serious. "There is a thief aboard my ship. I need your help."

"SIR REX AT YOUR SERVICE," roars the Inspector. "Tell me everything, Cap'n Joshua. I will get to work at once."

"Well," begins Cap'n Josh, "one thing has me puzzled..." A loud knock on the door interrupts him. In rushes Wrecker, Chief Engineer. He's so upset he forgets to close the door behind him.

"Chef Jambon just told me about the THIEF in the kitchen," cries Wrecker. "But that's not the ONLY place the thief has been. He's been in my ENGINE ROOM, too. Some of my tools are gone. He's robbed my tool chest!"

"This is getting spooky," Cap'n Josh says nervously. "I'll tell you everything that's happened so far. Then you can go to work AT ONCE, Sir Rex."

When Josh finishes describing the mysterious happenings, Sir Rex jumps up. "I must examine Miss Lola's cabin immediately. There may be fingerprints. Then I'll inspect the kitchen and the engine room…"

"AFTER THAT," cries Dr. Phineas, as he rushes through the open door, "you must come and have a look IN MY HOSPITAL."

"OH, NO," moans Cap'n Joshua, "you, TOO?"

"I'm afraid so, Cap'n Josh. Someone has stolen a dozen big boxes of cotton from my hospital supplies. What do you make of THAT? Why would anyone want to steal cotton?"

"Strange!" murmurs Sir Rex. "Crackers, peanut butter, chocolate fudge cake, jewels, engine room tools, cotton — what next?"

Then he roars, "CAP'N JOSHUA, YOU ARE RIGHT! This IS getting spooky! I must go to work immediately!" He rushes off to Lola's cabin.

As Lola opens the door, Sir Rex bows. "It's a pleasure to meet a beautiful and famous movie star like you, Miss Lola. I'm sorry your jewels have been stolen, but perhaps I can find them for you!"

Lola has been crying, but she smiles at the Inspector and begins to feel much better.

"Please come in," Lola sighs. And, pointing to her empty trunk, she says, "The thief broke the lock. Clever, wasn't he?"

"Indeed," answers Rex as he examines the lock. "Strange," he mumbles to himself, "no fingerprints—not a one. But what are these deep scratch marks?"

"What's wrong?" Lola asks nervously.

"I'm not sure." Sir Rex looks puzzled. "I need to know much, much more before I can solve this case. I must leave now. If anyone comes looking for me, I'll be with Chef Jambon."

As Sir Rex enters the kitchen, cooks and waiters are scurrying from one end of the big room to the other preparing for the costume ball tonight. Outsiders aren't welcome in the kitchen just now — everyone is too busy to be bothered with visitors. In fact, at this moment Chef Jambon is ordering Jack, the ship's Sports Director, to get out from underfoot.

Sometimes he lets Jack watch while the cakes are being decorated. But NOT TODAY! Today Chef Jambon is peevish and cross because of what's happened to his lovely chocolate fudge cake.

Jack laughs and says, "It could be worse — someone could have stolen your WHOLE cake instead of just the top." Jambon doesn't think Jack is funny. He continues to scowl. So Jack hurries off to meet Allie, one of the cruise passengers, who has promised to go jogging with him.

19

As Jack comes out on deck, Allie notices his mischievous grin and asks, "What have YOU been up to?"

Jack laughs and explains about Chef Jambon's cake with the missing top.

20

Allie frowns. "That's not ALL that's missing on board this ship. I tried to help find some books in the library today. But they've vanished just like the top of Chef Jambon's cake."

Jack is puzzled. "Here comes the Inspector. Let's tell him about the books. I heard him talking in the kitchen about a THIEF aboard our ship!"

But before Jack and Allie can report their news, Sir Rex says excitedly, "We're making progress! I've found strange fingerprints in the kitchen and in the hospital. I'm on my way to the engine room now to see if I can find strange fingerprints on Wrecker's tool chest. Cheerio!" He rushes toward the engine room stairs.

"BEASTLY WARM DOWN HERE, WRECKER!" Sir Rex shouts. The giant engines are making a terrific racket. The Inspector takes off his coat and hat and mops his face with a big handkerchief.

"If I worked down here in this heat," he says to himself, "I'd have to cut my handsome thick mane. What a pity that would be. Perhaps it's better for me to be a Chief Inspector than a Chief Engineer."

"FOLLOW ME, SIR, AND WATCH YOUR STEP," Wrecker shouts.

Sir Rex has never seen so much huge machinery — everything booming, churning, grinding, hissing or humming. He follows Wrecker and walks carefully to avoid being smeared with grease or oil. Nevertheless, he bumps into a barrel and gets a great glob of grease on his clothes. BUT WAIT!...

"THAT'S NOT GREASE!" roars Sir Rex. "That's chocolate fudge frosting! Our thief is hiding in YOUR ENGINE ROOM, WRECKER. Let's have a look."

They begin to search. Wrecker shouts, "MORE CHOCOLATE FUDGE FROSTING OVER HERE, SIR."

They find more and more smudges. Sir Rex explains, "Whoever stole the cake had a hard time carrying it. He couldn't see where he was going and just ran around in circles smearing chocolate all over everything— WHAT A MESS!"

"HOLD ON A MINUTE! LOOK AT THAT!" Sir Rex points at a bit of something fuzzy and white caught in a large metal drawer almost hidden behind some big pipes. "I think we've found our thief! Now be careful," he warns.

Slowly he pulls the big drawer open...

Sitting there in a pile of cracker
crumbs and reading peacefully is a
MOUSE! His ears are stuffed with cotton
to shut out the booming engine noises, and his
red and white T-shirt is smeared with fresh chocolate fudge frosting.

Startled, the mouse looks up into the Inspector's big eyes. He pulls
the wads of cotton from his ears, smiles pleasantly and squeaks…

"Buon Giorno! I'm Velvetino!"

"GET UP, VELVETINO!" Sir Rex roars. "THE CAPTAIN IS LOOKING FOR YOU!"

Velvetino tries to scamper over the side of the big drawer, but the Inspector grabs him by the tail. "Hold on there, my lad—not so fast! We're going to see the Captain."

Velvetino is not grinning now, as he stands before the scowling Cap'n Joshua.

"You are in very SERIOUS trouble—VERY, VERY serious trouble, Velvetino! You are not only a THIEF but a STOWAWAY as well." Cap'n Josh is angry.

"I can see that it is you who has been taking food from Chef Jambon's kitchen. Also, I understand why you took the boxes of cotton from Dr. Phineas's hospital and why Allie was unable to find some of our library books.

"WHAT I DO NOT UNDERSTAND," says Cap'n Josh, who is really angry now, "is WHY you took Wrecker's tools, broke into Miss Lola's trunk and STOLE HER JEWELS!"

Suddenly, Velvetino, who has been looking very ashamed, looks very frightened. He begins to tremble. "What's all this about tools and jewels? I DON'T UNDERSTAND, Cap'n Joshua!"

Velvetino stands as tall as he can, looks Cap'n Josh straight in the eye and squeaks, "It's true, sir, I have done some very bad things, but I'm telling the truth when I say I don't know ANYTHING about Wrecker's tools or Miss Lola's jewels. I want to work hard and pay for the trouble I've caused, so I can stay aboard the S.S. HAPPINESS and go to China with you. But PLEASE, PLEASE don't blame me for someone else's terrible mischief."

Sir Rex says, "I think our stowaway is telling the truth, Captain. He's a cheeky little chap — but he's not a jewel thief. We must, I fear, search for a far more DANGEROUS VILLAIN than Velvetino."

Velvetino sighs with relief. "Cap'n Joshua, I'll do anything you ask to make up for my foolish crimes."

"Hush now," orders the Inspector. "You can discuss your foolhardy behavior with Cap'n Joshua later. Right now we have IMPORTANT work to do."

Sir Rex takes out his pencil and notebook.

"First, all passengers must be warned that there is a DANGEROUS jewel thief on board. We must tell them to lock away their diamonds and money and be very, very cautious. THEIR LIVES MAY BE IN DANGER!"

WARNING
JEWEL THIEF
ON BOARD

COSTUME
BALL

TONITE

Cap'n Joshua is shocked.
"WHY DO YOU SAY
THAT?"

"Because," answers the
Inspector, "Miss Lola's jewels
are worth more than a million
dollars. Whoever stole them will
stop at nothing to keep from being caught.
I must work FAST! Lola may be in MORE DANGER than anyone!"

Again, Cap'n Josh exclaims, "WHY DO YOU SAY THAT?"

"I'll explain later," replies Sir Rex as he rushes out of the cabin and
heads for the engine room.

32

Wrecker is checking dials as the Inspector arrives.

"SHOW ME YOUR TOOL CHEST!" Sir Rex shouts to Wrecker.

As he examines the chest, Sir Rex exclaims, "Ah, just as I suspected! LOOK, WRECKER! See these deep scratch marks? They are just like the marks I found on Miss Lola's trunk. THEY WILL LEAD US TO THE THIEF!!!"

Sir Rex bolts up the stairs shouting, "I MUST SEE THE CAPTAIN AT ONCE!"

33

The Inspector is hurrying along the deck, when Lola, sitting beside the swimming pool, stops him.

"May I please have a word with you, Sir Rex?"

"My pleasure, Miss Lola."

"I want you to meet my new friends," Lola says. "Mr. and Mrs. Crunch, who have been so nice to me since we left San Francisco."

34

"Also, I want to know if you've any idea yet who stole my beautiful jewels?"

Sir Rex bows politely to Mr. and Mrs. Crunch. "Ah, at last we are introduced. I have seen you with Miss Lola many times and have been hoping to meet you." The Inspector would have been a gentleman and kissed Mrs. Crunch's hand, but she was too busy painting her long nails.

"As for your stolen jewels, Miss Lola, I am sorry that I have nothing to report just yet."

35

"You must be patient, Lola," advises Mr. Crunch. "I'm sure Sir Rex is doing everything he can to solve the mystery. He may know more than he's telling us. Right, Inspector?"

"Perhaps," answers Sir Rex. "Excuse me now. I have an appointment with Cap'n Joshua."

Josh is pacing back and forth. "You MUST do something, Sir Rex. Everyone aboard the S.S. HAPPINESS is frightened. No one knows where or when the mysterious thief will strike next. How can anyone have a good time at the costume ball tonight when they are so scared?"

"Don't worry, Cap'n Joshua! The mystery will be solved tonight before the party is over. Excuse me now. I must begin dressing. It takes time to get into my costume. Just remember what I said. STOP WORRYING!"

Sir Rex leaves the cabin— a secret smile on his face.

The S.S. HAPPINESS has a beautiful ballroom. Tonight it's filled with people dressed in every kind of costume. Everyone is dancing. They've eaten Chef Jambon's delicious party feast—including his famous chocolate fudge cake. Jambon is peeking through a crack in the kitchen door watching the fun.

38

Velvetino has disappeared
behind a mountain of soap
suds. He's hard at work washing
dishes, helping to make up
for the trouble he's caused.

In the ballroom Cap'n Joshua
is at a table with Allie,
Dr. Phineas, Jack, Tasha and
Wrecker. He's trying to have a good
time, but he can't stop worrying.

"The Inspector's a good dancer," Tasha
remarks as she watches Sir Rex whirl
by with Mrs. Crunch. "He's a real
gentleman, too. Why else would he ask
that clumsy, ugly lady to dance?"

Sir Rex is very uncomfortable.
Mrs. Crunch's long sharp nails are
scraping his hand. "If I weren't wearing
this metal armor," Rex thinks,
"she would be poking her horrible nails
into my back, as well as my hand."

40

41

As the music ends, Sir Rex hears someone behind him say, "What's THIS? Our famous Inspector is DANCING instead of searching for the DANGEROUS JEWEL THIEF? Perhaps you've already FOUND the villain, Inspector?"

Sir Rex spins around just as Mr. Crunch raises his hand to tap him on the shoulder.

42

SCRITCH—SCRATCH—SCREECH…it's the sound of Mr. Crunch's sharp nails as they hit the Inspector's arm.

Sir Rex doesn't answer Mr. Crunch's nasty teasing. Instead he stares at the long, ugly scratch that Mr. Crunch has made on the sleeve of his armor. He looks up and roars….

"YOU ARE CORRECT, MR. CRUNCH, I DO KNOW WHO THE THIEF IS! and so do YOU, Mr. and Mrs. Crunch!

"It was the two of you who stole the tools from Wrecker's engine room, so you could break open Miss Lola's trunk and steal her jewels.

"At first I didn't know who or what made those strange scratch marks. This afternoon I guessed it was you and Mrs. Crunch. NOW I HAVE PROOF!!!!"

Sir Rex points to the ugly scratch on his armor. "THIS is just as good as a fingerprint! I ARREST YOU, MR. AND MRS. CRUNCH, FOR STEALING MISS LOLA'S JEWELS!"

"I CAN'T BELIEVE IT," Lola cries. "They wanted to be my friends just so they could find out where I kept my jewels."

"RIGHT," roars Sir Rex. "I'm sure we'll find your jewels cleverly hidden away in their cabin. Your tools, Wrecker, are probably at the bottom of the ocean. I'm sure these crooks threw them overboard as soon as they forced open the trunk and took the jewels!"

"Take the Crunches to their cabin and lock them in!" orders Cap'n ~~~ua. "I'll send two guards to watch their door!"

45

Cap'n Joshua salutes Sir Rex, smiles at the crowd and cries, "START THE MUSIC — EVERYONE DANCE — THIS HAS TURNED INTO A REAL CELEBRATION. All we need now is another big chocolate fudge cake!"

46